Mythology Anthology

Four Short Stories

Edited by B. Heather Mantler

TABLE OF CONTENTS

THE WAR TORN
ALEXANDRA A. CHESHIRE

The small cloaked and hooded figure picks her way across the still smoking field. Small bare feet step over torn uniformed bodies and discarded weapons. As if by some mystical force, those bare feet are neither bloodied nor bruised by the detritus of war. The ground is littered with shell casings and ragged fragments of metal and sharp fragments of bone, but none of these touch the small bare feet as they pass over.

A river red with spilled blood cuts across the field, washing away but a tiny fragment of the chaos. The small figure stops on the bank, moss green eyes peering out from under the hood. Those eyes look first upstream, then down.

A harsh caw cuts across the otherwise silent field. With a flutter of wings, a large glossy black bird drops onto the bank opposite. Bright bird eyes study the small figure. The moss green eyes study the raven in return.

"This is no place for a child."

"There is no place for a child in this world." Frail hands rise to push back the hood of the cloak. The face revealed is equally frail, with thin pointed features. The moss green eyes appear too large. Curling tendrils of coppery hair frame the face and disappear down into the cloak.

"There is always a place for children."

"This world is hell bent on its own destruction."

"Only because those in power perceive only their insurmountable differences," The bright bird eyes are again studying the small figure, "But a change in perception is coming. Coming soon."

"Soon no one will be left."

"If you wish to preserve this world, find the last standing oak."

"There is an oak still standing?"

"Find the last standing oak before the day of the dead." The raven's wings extend. Two powerful strokes lift the bird high into the sky where it circles above the field.

On the ground below, the small cloaked figure pulls the hood back into place before turning a slow circle. Moss green eyes survey the the remnants of the battlefield. There is no sign of any other living thing.

"The last oak before the day of the dead." Now the words sound too loud in the stillness. The small figure shivers, pulling the cloak tighter. Slowly, one step at a time, the small bare feet retrace their path across the field.

The encampment is invisible to all but those who know of its existence. The canvas of the tents are coloured to camouflage with the surrounding barren mountainside. The few fires permitted are built of the driest fuel available. Any smell of cooking food is somehow dampened as are any sounds made by the residents. Even the smallest children present are nearly silent.

A small cloaked and hooded figure slips through the encampment. Small bare feet cross the ragged rocks of the mountainside as if they were smooth. None of the few others outside the tents pay any attention to the figure.

At the door of the center-most tent, a frail hand reaches up to touch the small bell hanging from a slender cord. No sound comes from it, but the tent flap soon moves aside enough to admit the cloaked figure.

Unlike the exterior, the interior of the tent is warm and vibrantly colourful. Soft rugs cover the ground and brilliant tapestries line the walls. Warmth is rolling off a small stove in the middle of everything. Low beds covered with bright blankets take up one side. Chests and shelves of all manner of items take up the other. At the very back is a small table with a chair on either side. One of those chairs is occupied by an ancient, frail woman wrapped in layer upon layer of shawls.

The small cloaked and hooded figure stops by one bed to shed the hooded cloak. Beneath that garment, which gets laid across the foot of the bed, there is a thin grey shift dress not quite to the knees. Wildly curly copper hair now cascades down a thin back. The girl herself is so frail looking she appears to have been recently ill and little recovered.

"Come sit and eat, girl," The ancient woman makes no effort to move, "And tell me what it was you saw today."

The girl obeys, helping herself to some dried foodstuffs and a mug of water before taking the chair opposite the woman. The first few minutes pass in silence while the girl eats. Only once she is less hungry does she look at the woman opposite.

"The battle is over," The words are matter of fact, in no way reflecting the horror of the battlefield, "None were left alive this time."

The ancient woman nods to herself, "An increasingly common tale of late. What else?"

"The raven came."

"Scald-Crow?" The ancient woman frowns in her surprise.

The girl nods.

"What did She say?"

"A change in perception is coming... if the last oak can be found before the day of the dead."

"The day of the dead is tomorrow," The frown deepens, "And there are no oak left."

The girl shrugs and returns to her food.

While she continues to eat, the ancient woman eases herself to her feet and begins moving around the tent. From one shelf, she takes an old hard bound book. From a chest, she takes a folded cloth. From another chest, she takes several stones. From a second shelf, she takes a small chalice. Each item gets set on the table.

"If you've finished eating, go play. I've work to do."

The girl slips from her chair, takes the now empty mug to a stand containing other mugs, reclaims her cloak and leaves the tent. Just outside, she pauses to fasten the cloak around her neck and pull her hood up over her bright hair.

Slipping silently uphill through the tents, the girl begins to climb the mountain. Nimble fingers and bare feet easily scale the barren rock.

It is not a large mountain, barely big enough to be worthy of the name, and it does not take the girl long to reach the small plateau at the very top. Up there, she sits with her feet tucked under her to survey the surrounding land.

Battle after battle in a seemingly endless war has left the countryside a blasted, muddy mess. Forests have been either chopped down and hauled away for mysterious purposes or blasted with chemicals until all the foliage is gone. Swamps have expanded to take over fields, aided by relentless rains. While no rain is currently falling on the mountain, ominous clouds hang in the sky above. The girl seated on the mountain top can see for kilometres in all directions and in none of them can she see a living tree.

What she can see is the approach of more uniformed men accompanied by more of their war machines. There only appears to be one group, but they are rapidly nearing the hidden camp. Drawing a deep breath, the girl lets loose a warning howl, then a second and a third. She slips off the plateau and scrambles down the mountain as fast as she dares move.

The camp is all but gone by the time the girl slides the last short distance. Only the center-most tent remains and the ancient woman is standing in the entrace, waving to the girl to hurry. Small bare feet slip and slide across the rock in her haste. As soon as she is close, the girl dives into the tent, curling into a ball on the floor as the ancient woman allows the flap to drop.

As the girl huddles on the tent floor, her eyes squeezed closed, the world tilts sideways. Her stomach also tilts sideways. However, the girl is used to the sensation and does her best to ride it out until the world around her settles.

She spends a moment just allowing herself to relax before opening her eyes. Slowly, she uncurls from her position on the floor and eases herself to her feet. Looking around, she spots the ancient woman sprawled on the tent floor not far away. Frowning in concern, the girl goes to examine the woman.

As she does that, another woman, a younger one, slips inside the tent. She glances around before coming over to the girl.

"Is she alive?"

The girl shakes her head, "She was working a ritual when the warning sounded. She didn't have the strength."

The younger woman's shoulders slump and she sighs, "We won't be safe here long. The armies are everywhere."

The girl slowly straightens up, her green eyes passing over the contents of the tent.

"Did she teach you anything?" The younger woman also straightens up, "What ritual was she working even?"

"Our only hope," The words come slowly, "Is for one of us to find the last oak by the day of the dead."

"That's no hope at all. The day of the dead is nearly upon us and there are no oak left."

The girl shrugs, "The words are the raven's."

The younger woman swallows hard, "I suppose it must be possible then. 'Though I don't see how."

Silence falls over the tent for a short time. Then the girl draws in a deep breath, straightening her shoulders.

"Take care of her. I must go."

Before the woman can stop her, the girl slips away, out of the tent and through the camp.

Instead of being on a mountainside, the camp is now in the depths of a swamp, the tents arranged on the limited patches of solid ground remaining. The girl is cautious as she makes her way across the murky ground, her bare feet picking their way from solid earth to solid earth.

Without any real direction or destination, the girl keeps herself moving as the remaining daylight fades. The moon rises early, allowing her enough light to continue on, but once it sets, she is forced to stop and rest until dawn.

Having left the swamp far behind, the girl is now out in the open, her only source of concealment her cloak. She huddles down in it in the pitch dark, praying to every deity she knows of for safety and guidance.

The first light of dawn comes with the sound of booted feet marching ever closer. The girl pulls her cloak tightly around herself as she scrambles to her feet and flees across the war torn wasteland. In her panic, she barely notices the changes in the land around her until she trips over a tree root and collides with the rough, thick trunk.

The girl slumps down, again pulling her now ragged cloak tight around her. Moss green eyes widen as they take in her surroundings. After a moment, she shivers down further into her cloak.

"Child?" The voice is light and feminine.

Blinking, the girl looks up at a tall cloaked figure with a hood pulled low. It is impossible to discern anything about face or figure. She presses her back against the tree.

"I mean you no harm."

The girl pulls her cloak tighter around herself.

"How did you get here?"

The girl only huddles down further into her cloak, aware of the shaded eyes studying her. A moment later, surprisingly strong arms scoop up the girl and carry her away from the tree. She remains as tightly huddled into her cloak as she can, even when finally set down on a far softer surface than any she has ever felt.

"A child?" This new voice is deeper, but still feminine.

"So it would seem. She appeared at the sacred oak."

"Appeared? Well, the barriers between worlds are at their thinnest today. Has she said anything?"

"No."

A harsh caw sounds in the distance. A second caw comes louder, as if the source is coming closer. A third is even closer and sounds somehow familiar to the huddled and shivering girl. Hesitantly, she peeks around the edge of her hood.

She is in the center of a circle of large trees, laying on a thick blanket. Everything around her is the green and brown of a healthy forest. Nearby, two tall cloaked and hooded figures are watching as a large glossy raven lands on the ground beside the blanket.

"Child, you have succeeded in your first task."

"My first task?" The girl's voice is hesitant.

"Task?" The lighter of the two feminine voices sounds curious.

The raven ignores the tall cloaked figures, "Now you need to find the means to change perception and return by the end of the day."

"By the end of the day?"

"Fail and you will be unable to return." The raven's wings spread. Two strokes and the bird is gone.

"The means to change perception?" The deeper voice sounds concerned.

"Return where?" The other tall figure moves to crouch beside the girl.

Her face loses any expression and vanishes under her hood.

"You have met this raven before?" The lack of response elicits a frustrated sigh, "We could aid you, if you would only tell us what it is you need."

"Aid costs." The words are muffled by the hood.

"Our aid costs nothing. But if you've a task set by the raven, you need to accept aid freely offered."

The girl remains motionless long after the words die away into silence. Then, slowly, hesitantly, frail hands appear to push back the hood.

"Have you been ill, child?" Concern enters the lighter voice.

The girl slowly shakes her head.

"Are you starved then?"

A confused frown flickers over the girl's face.

"Have you had enough to eat?"

The question elicits a half shrug as the girl eases herself to sitting.

"Perhaps it's more a question of what she's been eating... or rather hasn't been eating," The deeper voice observes, "Considering her arrival and her clothes, I doubt she's from any local village."

"Village?" The confused frown returns.

"The raven said you need to find 'the means to change perception'," The lighter voice recalls, "Perception of what? Whose perception of what?"

"Those in power perceive only their insurmountable differences." The girl recalls out loud.

"A conflict then?" The deeper voice sounds surprised.

"War," The girl's voice drops to nearly inaudible, "It's been going on as long as I can remember. Maybe as long as I've been alive."

"War?" The two hooded figures glance at each other.

"After my parents were killed, I was apprenticed to the wise woman who kept our camp hidden from the armies. But she died and if the camp is found, no one will be left alive," The words tumble over one another, growing louder, "Supplies were running low and the land is dying. The raven thinks we have hope, but..."

"If the raven thinks you have hope, then hope you have," The deeper voice is firm, "You're here and you have our help."

"I only have today." Worry creeps into the words.

"Then we will have to hurry."

"But what are we looking for? You've been given a very nonspecific description which could refer to almost anything."

"What started such a war? Do you know, child?"

The girl starts to shrug, then frowns, "There is a story I heard once... a valuable, ancient chalice was stolen... or at least vanished. The two sides blamed each other."

"A chalice?" The two cloaked figures exchange glances, "An ancient and valuable chalice?"

"Could such a thing have been transported as this girl was?"

"But would returning the chalice help now?" The girl looks from one to the other, "It's been so many years."

"I think it likely the chalice has some power. Else why fight over it so long?"

"So where would such a thing be? A chalice of any power would be either hidden away from all or in the hands of a single person."

"I wonder..." The girl eases herself to her feet, moss green eyes scanning her surroundings. After a moment, she pulls her hood back over her hair.

"You think you know something, child?"

"Could a powerful chalice hide itself?" The girl does not wait for an answer, instead walking to a gap in the trees on the far side of the circle. Once she is between the trees, she pauses to scan the area again. Then her eyes close and she turns in a slow circle.

"Child?" The deeper voice is both curious and concerned.

"Like calls to like," The soft words carry surprisingly strongly, "I am of the chalice's world."

"You think only one of your world could find it?" There is no surprise in the lighter voice.

"An effective means of hiding," The deeper voice sounds bemused, "We will aid your return to the sacred oak when you have found the chalice."

The girl nods once, quickly before slipping away through the trees. Now she knows what she is looking for and how to find it, her bare feet carry her unerringly towards the object of her quest.

The forest soon meets up with a sheer stone wall, with little room for even a slender girl to slip through the space between the trees and the rock. Around a corner, she finds the opening to a shallow cave. At first glance, the cave is empty, but the girl steps inside anyway. When she reaches the center of the small space, she turns in a slow circle, her eyes scanning the walls around her. All she can see is bare rock.

A long, low whistle above her causes the girl to look up. Spotting a hole in the stone of the ceiling, she moves until she can see more clearly into it. In the light from the cave entrance, she can just make out a shadowy shape set on a narrow ledge. It is too high up for her to be able to jump to it and the cave walls are too smooth for any attempt at climbing. A frown appears as the girl considers the problem.

Leaving the cave, she turns her eyes up the rock wall and soon spots a section rough enough for her to climb. Nimbly, she climbs up and is able to find the top end of the hole in the cave roof surprisingly easily. The opening at the top is narrow, but not too narrow for the girl's thin body. Her bare feet slip in first, followed by the rest of her, and she wriggles her way down. The space is tight, making her feel as though it is hard to breathe, but she keeps moving, her entire focus on reaching the item on the ledge below. When she reaches it, the space is too tight for her to just pick it up to take with her. Instead, she has to drop down into the cave, only her fingers left clinging to the ledge. From this precarious position, she can just barely use one hand to knock the item off the ledge. It falls down beside her with a clatter of metal on stone. The girl drops after it, landing lightly beside the large, tarnished metal cup.

Picking up the chalice, the girl studies it with a deepening frown. Nothing about it suggests any value or power beyond that of an ordinary drinking cup. With a slightly irritated sigh, the girl takes the cup and leaves the cave, retracing her steps back to the circle of trees where the two cloaked and hooded figures are waiting.

"You'll have to hurry, child," The deeper voice sounds concerned, "The day of the dead is nearly over and you still need to return to the sacred oak."

The girl only nods.

"Follow me." The owner of the lighter voice guides the girl out of the circle of trees. The girl follows closely, the chalice clutched tightly in her hands.

The sun is nearly to the western horizon when the taller of the two cloaked and hooded figures stops beside the largest tree in the forest.

"This is the sacred oak."

The girl nods, still clutching the chalice. Resolutely, she places one bare foot in front of the other, aiming directly for the thick trunk. Even though she is walking slowly, a tree root seems to rise up to trip her. She falls headlong into the trunk and ends up rolling forward onto blasted, blackened field.

A harsh caw and a flutter of wings do nothing to help the girl's disorientation as she blinks in the dreary grey light.

"You found the chalice."

The girl rolls onto her side and finds herself nose to beak with a large glossy raven. She scrambles back, one hand retaining a tight hold on the metal cup.

"Take it to the river's head."

"River?"

Glossy wings spread, flap twice and the raven is airborne. A moment later, the bird is gone from sight.

Still clutching the chalice, the girl eases herself to her feet, her eyes scanning the wasteland around her. There is no sign of the oak or any other tree on the flat, open field.

"What river?" The girl shivers, her eyes now going to the metal of the chalice.

The sky is growing darker as she sets out walking without a

specific direction in mind.

About the time exhaustion and complete darkness threaten to engulf the girl, she stumbles into the ruins of a tiny hut. Just enough of the old structure is standing for her to curl up in her cloak, the chalice gripped tightly in her hands. Her empty stomach growls and she does her best to ignore it. The silence of the black night and the wasteland press in on her. She huddles closer in on herself, fighting to relax enough to rest even a little.

A grey and rainy dawn finds her stumbling to her feet, half asleep and still hungry. The girl presses on in her chosen direction, the part of her mind not numbed by her circumstances hoping to find her destination by luck. One bare foot drags behind the other across a landscape which does not seem to change in the slightest all through the long, grey, rainy day.

Just as the daylight is fading to night, the girl stumbles over the rougher ground at the base of barren foothills. More by instinct than design, her bare feet find a path leading up through the hills to full mountains. Still by instinct, her feet remain on the path even as the blackness of an overcast night settles in. Her eyes are useless in the utter darkness. Numbed hands keep shifting their grip on the chalice to reassure the girl she has not lost it. When exhaustion overtakes her next, she collapses on the path and is unaware of anything until a harsh cawing cuts through the haze of deep sleep.

As the girl blinks away her disorientation, she becomes aware of daylight and glossy black feathers. She eases herself to sitting, her fingers fumbling around for some half remembered object.

"The chalice is here," The raven directs the girl's gaze with its beak, "And your destination is just over the next ridge. Meet me there." A sweep of wings carries the bird away.

The girl remains seated for long moments, her mind seemingly unable to come fully awake. At last, she picks herself up, retrieves the chalice and continues to follow the path up.

At the top of the ridge, she can see down to a large pool of clear water surrounded by rocky bank on three sides. On the fourth, the waters rush away down the mountain to form a river. Three people are standing on the bank, two male and one female.

The men are dressed in different uniforms and eyeing each other with hostility. The woman is standing a little apart and wearing little more than the long bright red hair draped over and around her body.

The girl swallows hard, her hands clutching the chalice tighter, as she follows the path down to the bank. She is painfully aware of all three sets of eyes on her as her bare feet carry her to the water's edge.

"Dip the chalice and drink, child." The woman's voice is strong and commanding.

Hesitantly, the girl crouches down to fill the metal cup with water. She wraps both hands around it as she brings it to her lips. At the first sip, she feels washed clean of the exhaustion and hunger which have been constant companions since she had left her home camp.

"Fill the chalice again and bring it here."

The girl obeys, this time without any hesitation.

The red woman addresses the men, "Both of you will drink. And we will see once and for all which of you is mightier."

Both men look as if they would like to protest, but something in the woman's gaze keeps them silent. The girl presents one of them with the full chalice. As soon as he has taken a sip, the girl takes it back to present to the other man. Again, once he has taken a sip, the girl takes back the chalice.

"Sit there." The woman points the girl to a small shelf in the nearby rock. The girl goes, taking the chalice with her, to sit and watch as the two men continue to stare each other down.

Neither moves except to draw himself up into an ever more rigid, more defiant posture. Both appear to grow taller. Or at least until they collapse to the ground, curling in on themselves like tiny, frightened children. After a time, one ceases to move at all, while the other slowly straightens out and sits up. The seated man's eyes are wide as he looks around as if seeing the place for the first time. Then his gaze lands on the red woman.

"Who...?" He swallows hard.

"It is time to end the conflict and renew the land and people," Her gaze seems to pierce right through him, "Else there will be nothing to renew."

The man straightens up, defiance returning to his posture,

"There can be no end to the conflict while..."

"Look," The woman cuts him off, one arm gesturing toward the girl, "Do you not understand just how few children are left? How few mothers are left to bear and raise them? There is a time for destruction and a time for renewal. You survived your sip from the chalice," Now her hand moves towards the too still figure on the ground, "Do you think you would survive a second?"

"The child survived."

"Because she is a child."

"What is this chalice?"

"A means to change perception. If indeed there is any means to such a change. Think on it." A swirl of red resolves itself into glossy black feathers as a large raven flies away from the mountain.

The man remains still, studying the body opposite him. Then his eyes turn to the girl seated on the stone shelf. He studies what can be seen of the hooded and cloaked figure for a time before he picks himself up off the ground and takes a step towards her.

"Who are you?"

Thin shoulders shrug indifferently.

He frowns, concern appearing in his face, "Where are you from?"

Again, an indifferent shrug.

"Where is your family?"

"Dead." There is a flat finality to the word. Abruptly, the girl stands, spilling the remaining water out of the chalice. Her hands retain their grip on the cup as she walks towards the path by which she had come to the pool.

"Where are you going?" The man calls after her.

The only response is an indifferent shrug of thin shoulders as bare feet pace towards the top of the ridge and the path down the other side.

Alexandra A. Cheshire

PANDORA'S BOX
B. HEATHER MANTLER

Earth 1990 (Second Row, Fifth Book)

The two teenaged boys wandered around the old, antique shop studying the shelves that were stuffed full of various, dust covered objects.

"Man, Mr. Aristro keeps some strange stuff in here," Andrew said almost in awe.

"I wonder who he sells some of this stuff to that he makes a living out of this shop," James queered.

"Probably the tourists who pass through during the summer months. I've seen two or three buy things here. They don't stay too long, but they do buy things," Andrew replied.

"With the amount of dust in this place it's a wonder anyone could stand this place for that long," James said.

"Mr. Aristro is probably used to it. Some days I think he's as old as some of the stuff that's in here."

"Tell me about it, he still wears a full suit every day, I mean the kind with vest and suspenders. That went out of fashion last century. Did he tell you where he was going or how long we were suppose to mind the store?"

"All he said was that he had an emergency somewhere else that he had to see to."

"What kind of emergency? All he has is this junk shop."

"I didn't ask."

After looking around a few more minutes Andrew sat down on the stool behind the counter, while James continued to wander the shop.

"Drew, come look at this," James said from the doorway to the back of the shop. Andrew got up and followed James to the back of the shop. There on a table sat an old, wooden chest with the words carved into the top 'do not open.' "I wonder what's inside that's you're not suppose to open it."

"Well, the best way to find out is to open it."

"You aren't seriously thinking about opening it, are you?"

"Sure, adults have all sorts of secrets we're not suppose to know, but if you don't pry you don't learn anything." Andrew moved to stand right in front of the box, and started to open the lock.

"You're crazy, man." The lock came open easily in Andrew's hand and then the lid flew open with a strong gust of wind coming from the box, which blew the boys right off their feet. Andrew and James were almost thrown across the floor and into the wall. Andrew was the first of the boys to recover and quickly helped James to his feet.

"I told you to leave it alone," James said dusting himself off.

"Maybe. I'm trying to figure out what happened," Andrew responded. As the boys turned toward the chest a lady stepped out. Her ivory black hair fell down her back like water, her dainty feet were fitted with lavender shoes, and she wore a beautiful, lavender dress that fit snugly on her thin figure with a white lace shawl draped over her slim shoulders. The woman's porcelain looking face had a strange expression seemingly painted there. Neither boy could speak.

"You are the ones that freed me?" her words seemed to flow like sweet wine. Andrew nodded slightly. "I thank you," the woman tilted her head down a little and then slowly with the grace of nothing else on earth started towards the door. At that moment Mr. Aristro appeared in the doorway. He surveyed the scene and seemed to take every little detail in.

"Well, Andrew, I see you have opened Pandora's box again," he said. To this the lady sat down on a chair that was near her in a very unladylike manner.

"Nicholas, I figured you'd come around just in time to stop me from leaving as usual," the lady said with a sigh.

"Pandora, you should never leave your box. Andrew, since you let her out once again you will have to close the box," Mr. Aristro stated.

"How do I do that?" Andrew asked having no idea what Mr. Aristro or Pandora was talking about.

"You have to say the spell to close Pandora's box," Mr. Aristro replied tiredly.

"I don't know any spells," responded Andrew feeling scared.

"Why don't you try anything you can come up with?" Pandora suggested. Andrew gulped and began to say anything that came to mind that might work as a spell to close Pandora's box, not fully understanding what he was doing.

Pandora slowly felt herself grow stronger. She knew what would happen once she was up to full strength, but all she cared about was getting back into her box.

Andrew took up an hour and a half trying to find the right words to close the box and every time he thought he got it nothing happened. Finally, Pandora stood up,

"This world is the one with the shortest life."

Immediately following this was a large flash of light and the earth became a barren wasteland. The only things left were a small seedling, an old wooden box with the words 'Do Not Open' carved in the top and a middle-aged man wearing a black cloak.

"Don't worry Pandora, your box will be safe," said Nicholas Aristro.

Earth 2000 (Four Rows, Twentieth Book)
Dimension Six

Epimetheus hauled the old, wooden chest into the room. "Look what I found in the storage closet."

"What is in it?" asked Athena.

"I don't know," answered Epimetheus.

"Something dangerous," suggested Ares.

"Why would you say that?" asked Athena.

"Because the box says do not open," Ares responded.

"Knowing Prometheus, he'd write that on anything to keep

people out," said Epimetheus.

"True, but one day you'll find something that should have been left alone," Ares predicted.

"Yeah, right," Epimetheus laughed. He opened the lid of the chest and let the lid fall backwards out of his hands. "It's empty, why carve do not open on an empty box?"

Suddenly a wind blew from inside the box, blowing everybody at least five feet away from it. Out of the box stepped a lady, her black hair was braided and wrapped around her head, the emerald dress she wore seemed to shimmer like water as she moved and her nicely tanned face had a look of disgust upon it.

"Why did you have to open my box, again?" the woman demanded angrily.

"And you would be?" asked Epimetheus.

"Pandora," she answered. Epimetheus gulped.

"You know Ares, you could've picked a better time to be right," Epimetheus said as he got to his feet.

"If I could pick any other day to be right I would have," Ares replied.

"You still didn't answer my question," Pandora stated, irritated.

"I didn't know it was your box, I was just cleaning out the storage closet," Epimetheus answered. Just then Zeus entered the room.

"A glorious day today don't you think?" he asked.

"I think it was a nice day to stay inside and watch the war, famine and disease that was just let out," Pandora said as she brushed past Zeus and out of the room.

"Who was that?" Zeus asked looking after Pandora.

"That was Pandora straight out of her box," said Ares.

"Oh. So, who wants to go people watching?" asked Zeus happily.

Earth 2003 (Four Rows, Twentieth Book)
Main Dimension (Monday)

"Teresa, you'll never guess what?" Tabitha said as she came down the school hallway towards her best friend.

"There's a new guy in school and you think he's hot," Teresa guessed.

"How did you know?" Tabitha asked disappointed.

"You're predictable and I saw him well I was in the office talking to the principal," Teresa answered as she closed her locker and put the lock on it.

"And you didn't tell me?" Tabitha asked, as the girls walked toward the science labs.

"He has the same schedule as you, so I figured you'd see him before I had a chance to tell you."

"Talking about classes, did you finish your homework on the theorem Mr. Johnson was yammering on about yesterday?"

"Yes, but I'm not lending it to you to copy."

"Why not?"

"Because science class starts in two minutes, you'll never have time to finish copying my notes and then Mr. Johnson will catch you and we'll both get a zero on the assignment. This way only you get zero."

"Thanks a lot."

"You're welcome." The two girls entered the science lab and sat down.

Jason had been to this new school for a week and already he thought the whole school was bonkers. Sebastian, even though he had a girlfriend, chased girls and he treated everyone as if they were lower beings then himself. Lillian, Sebastian's girlfriend, was jealous of every other girl in the school. Alexander was a straight A student that only seemed to want to talk about fish and water wild life. Cyril, he isn't negative about things, just morbid. Minerva is really into toughness and fighting. Damon is another straight A student, the perfect teacher's pet. Selena is a nature freak and a vegetarian. Cynthia is the school beauty; her boyfriend is Iggy and if rumour is true occasionally sleeps with Gregory. Dennis is the prankster and joker of the school. Gregory is a loner and into picking fights with anyone. You would think he and Minerva would get along but they don't. Ignatius or Iggy from the smell of him hasn't figured out what soap in let alone how to use it; the question that hangs in most minds is how he got Cynthia as his girlfriend. Tabitha has a crush on just about every guy at school. Andrew is impulsive. Mr. Aristro is the librarian who has to be at least a hundred years old. Teresa seems to be the only normal, whatever that is at this school, person around.

Jason learned a school tradition that happens every Wednesday. A large group of girls keep a box in an empty locker and call it Pandora's box. Every week they open this box and take out the piece of paper inside which usually has two names typed on it, one male and one female. Because only three people know the combination of the lock and no one that knows it opens the locker during the week the group assumes that some magical being is putting these names in there and those two people are destined to be together. Stephen and Tim informed Jason that should his name come up in the box not to go out with the other person whose name was in the box. After several very bad dates the guys of the school had decided to ignore what Pandora's box says.

Earth 2003 (Four Rows, Twentieth Book)
Dimension Six

"What do you think of the new guy at school on the main dimension?" asked Apollo.

"He's too normal for the school," Aphrodite replied barely looking up from her compact mirror.

Looking up from his magazine Zeus asked, "What new guy?"

"He's afraid that he has got into too deep of water to swim," Poseidon commented as he feed his fish.

"I have not given him much thought as he is still alive," Hades said.

"He doesn't have enough muscle," Athena said.

"He probably wouldn't know how to fight anyways," Ares responded to Athena.

"How about you, Pandora?" Apollo asked.

"What?" asked Pandora looking up from her book.

"What do you think of the new guy, Jason?" Apollo asked again.

"He knows more then he lets on and he smells of a strange magic," Pandora answered.

"What kind of magic?" asked Apollo.

"I'm not sure but give it time I'll figure it out eventually,"

Pandora answered.

Earth 2003 (Four Rows, Twentieth Book)
Main Dimension (Thursday)

Jason was sitting at the top of the staircase during his spare when he saw Teresa and Tabitha in the hallway headed for Teresa's locker.

"So, Brian and Chloe are thinking of breaking up because Brian caught Chloe kissing Sebastian yesterday," Tabitha was telling Teresa.

"One day Sebastian will find himself in big trouble and Lillian will leave him there and find some one new," Teresa said.

"I doubt it. Lillian has never been interested in other guys," Tabitha replied.

"Maybe they were married in another life and are destined to be together no matter what?" Teresa suggested.

"Since when have you believed in other life stuff?"

"Never, it was just a suggestion."

"Whatever. Anyway, Chris promised to meet me in the library to work on our socials project."

"See ya later." Teresa watched as Tabitha disappeared around the corner, then opened the lock to the almost empty locker beside hers that the one group of girls keeps Pandora's box in. Jason watched Teresa take out the box and switch the paper with one in her pocket. Teresa then placed the box back in the locker.

"So, you're Pandora," Jason said in a lowered, but not a whisper voice, as Teresa put the lock back on the locker. Once she was finished Teresa looked up.

"Yes, I am. But I ask you not to tell anyone," Teresa responded.

"I won't tell anyone, but why do you do it?" Jason asked.

"It started as a joke and someone took it seriously and now it's the ultimate prank."

"As in you have an accomplice?"

"Dennis types the papers up and I put them into the box. It was his idea, but he couldn't figure out how to open the box."

"Looks easy enough."

"It's not, I created the box, sold it and someone else bought it. It has a security alarm. If you try to open the box without turning off the alarm the whole school will hear it."

"Anyone ever tried to open it?"

"How do you think I know the whole school will hear it?"

"Oh, just out of curiosity, who is it for next week?"

"You and Selena." Teresa said with a smile and then walked away.

Earth 2003 (Four Rows, Twentieth Book)
Dimension Six

Epimetheus stood at the front of the room with Pandora's box at his feet, while Pandora leaned against the wall to his left. Prometheus sat on a chair just behind Epimetheus. Zeus, Hera, Poseidon, Hades, Athena, Apollo, Artimis, Aphrodite, Hermes, Ares, Hepaestus all stood in the middle of the room where they had been asked to be. Epimetheus addressed the group,

"I made a mistake and I ask that I be allowed to correct it."

"And which mistake is this?" Hades asked. Pandora rolled her eyes.

"I opened Pandora's box letting loose disease, famine, war and Pandora. I realize now that it was a mistake," Epimetheus replied.

"Oh, that mistake, I didn't think that one turned out too bad," Hades said.

"Considering all the people that have been dying lately, you wouldn't be complaining." Artimis said to Hades.

"Anyway," Epimetheus said trying to get the group back on the subject, "It is up to you to decide whether I'm allowed to try to close Pandora's box."

The group looked at each other and Zeus spoke up, "Give us a little while to talk it out." Epimetheus nodded and left the room followed by Prometheus and Pandora. Once the door was closed Pandora sat down against the wall in the hallway.

"They're going to let you try to close the box," Pandora stated.

"How would you know?" asked Epimetheus.

"Because I know," Pandora answered.

Two hours later Zeus called them back into the room.

"The decision has been made," Zeus started, "we have

decided to allow you to try to put Pandora back in her box on the basis that the war, famine, and disease go with her."

"Okay, I think I can do that," Epimetheus replied.

Pandora sat there looking bored and the others had already left an hour ago. Epimetheus was staring at the box trying to figure out where the spell went wrong; he knew it had been the right spell.

"Quit moping around will you, I have better things to do than sit here and watch you," Pandora said finally.

"Tell me what happened with the spell," demanded Epimetheus.

"You did everything right. It will eventually put me back in the box," Pandora said before leaving.

Earth 2003(Four Rows, Twentieth Book)
Main Dimension (Friday)

The hallways were packed as the students rushed to their third class. Teresa didn't rush anywhere, as this block was her spare. Tabitha was in the library with Chris 'working' on the social studies project that they turned in last week. The hall was almost empty when Teresa finally got into her locker. She pulled out a binder and shut the locker, turning around she found Gregory standing in the empty hallway pointing a gun at her.

"You were suppose to go back yesterday," he said before pulling the trigger. Teresa felt the bullet enter her chest and collapsed. Footsteps could be heard as people came running to see what happened. "Now you're gone forever."

"Don't be too sure," Teresa got up, "You can't kill Pandora," Gregory looked shocked. So did Jason, who was the first one on the scene.

"How can you still be alive?" asked Gregory.

"The same reason I can't go back in my box. The world hasn't ended yet," Teresa answered.

"What has that got to do with it?" asked Gregory. Teresa breathed out a deep sigh.

"Once Andrew opens the box only he can close it, and each time he tries to close it I gain the energy, which I store. He does this five times; I get enough power and destroy the world. Only then do I go back into my box to sit and wait till the Andrew in the next world opens the box," Teresa said warily.

"Is there any way to prevent this from happening?" asked Jason. As others found the hallway blocked by some sort of invisible wall.

"I've had the box painted shut, glued shut, coffin nailed, curses put on it, a padlock without a key, and even more, he still opens the box." Teresa responded, "As for the world ending, since the process has already been started you can't stop it. I've tried everything I can think of to stop it, because ending the world gets boring after while."

"You can't be killed. How about going back in time and making sure Andrew doesn't find the box?" suggested Jason.

"I don't have enough energy for that," Teresa replied.

"How about a spell to stop the process?" asked Jason as Gregory went over to the wall banged his head on it once and then sat down with his back to it. Cyril, Minerva, Lillian, Alexander, Andrew and Dennis came through the invisible wall to see if they could help.

"No, any spell would just bounce right off me," Teresa answered.

"If Andrew didn't try to close the box?" Jason tried another suggestion.

"I will still drain power from him but it would just take longer," Teresa replied.

"What about if he didn't try to close your box in the first place?" Jason asked.

"Andrew has already tried to close the box," Teresa said confused.

"Yes, I know. But what if he hadn't?" Jason asked again.

"Then nothing would have happened, but he already tried," Teresa replied more confused as before.

"Then there is a solution," Jason said, "You go back in time to before Andrew tried to close the box and convince him that closing the box will end the world." Teresa thought about that for a few minutes then nodded.

Earth 2003 (Four Rows, Twentieth Book)
Main Dimension (Thursday)

Jason woke up to find himself in his own bed, not sure whether it was a dream or not he got up. His watch said it was six a.m. on Thursday. Jason got dressed and put on his shoes and coat. If it had all been a dream he would find out soon enough. He walked by the school to find Teresa sitting on the curb in front smoking a cigarette. He sat down beside her.

"Did my solution work?" he asked her. She nodded. "Then why do I remember what happened?"

"Because anyone inside the barriers remembers it," she answered without looking at him.

"It feels more like a dream."

"I don't think I've ever had a dream, but it's hard to remember everything that happened over the number of worlds that have come and gone."

"Is Andrew always the person who opens the box?"

"Yes, just like Nicholas is always the keeper of my box."

"Who is Nicholas?"

"The aged librarian."

"What are you going to do now?"

"Finish high school, go to college, and probably find cures to most of the diseases that got let out. Probably get lung cancer, mouth cancer and whatever else that comes with my habit of smoking."

"Why did you form that disgusting habit?"

"When you have seen what I have and done what all I've done you need something to do that's new. Besides, once I go back into my box my health goes back to perfect."

"Must be nice."

"Yeah, it is, too bad it only works for me." Jason got up as Teresa finished saying this.

"I have to get back home and get some more sleep if I'm going to be able to stay awake during class." Jason turned and started walking then stopped, turning around he said,

"Oh, yeah, one more thing."

"What's that?"

"Please don't put my name into the prank Pandora's Box."

B. Heather Mantler

THE SOUNDS OF WEATHER
HELEN DYCK

At a time long ago, there was a terrible hag of Scottish birth. She carried much evil in her and road the skies in a black chariot, pulled by three headed dragon. She would cross the skin in a cloud of darkness. She was almost invisible in this cloud. As she crossed the sky, she caused floods, ruined homes and crops, sickened the people and animals of the kingdom. The beautiful and loving queen of the kingdom of Annan put forth a cry for help from any of the kingdom's heroes to save her and her people. For the one brave enough to stand up to the evil hag, the queen promised she would take this hero as her husband. The hero would have power, riches, and all he desired to give him a long, happy and peaceful life by her side. Peter was a poor but very kind peasant. He was much in love with his queen but didn't think he even had a chance to be with her. Now Peter was the brave one to step forward to save the queen and the kingdom. Peter has a golden spear and had a magic spell put on the spear that could kill the hag. The next time the hag came across the sky, Peter was waiting for her. Peter had all the people and their animals hide in a cave. When the evil hag did not see any people or animals, she stuck her head and shoulders out of the darkened cloud. As she looked around, Peter was able to see her and throw his golden spear. Peter wounded the hag and she raced off in fear, never to be seen again.

The beautiful queen and Peter lived very happily ever after. As a reminder to always have hope a powerful fairy made the darkened clouds into a warning of a storm coming. The golden spear became lightning and the loud noises from the chariot and the dragon's passage became the thunder of the storm. The fairy said "Remember, you shall have happiness too"…Sleep now my child.

Os sons do Tempo

Nunha epoca na que hai moiton tempo, houbo unha terrible bruxa de nacemento Scotish. Ela levou moi mal nos seus e estradas os ceos nun coche negro, levado por unha drogon de tres cabezas. La cruzar o ceo nunha nube de escuridade. Ela era case invisible nesa nube. Mentres atravesaba o ceo, ela causou inundacions, casas e plantacions destruidas, e anoxado as persoas e os animals do reino. A Raina fermosa e amorosa do Kindom de Annan poner diante dun grito de axuda de calquera dos heroes do kingom para salvala e seu pobo. Ao valente dabindo para afrontar a bruxa mala, a raina prometeu que tomaria este heroe como o seu marido. O heroe teria poder, riquezas,e todo o que el desexaba darlie unha vida longa, feliz e en paz a beira dela. Peter era un campesino podre, pero moi amable. Era moinamorado coa sua raina, pero non creo que ainda tivo a oportunidade de estar con ela. Ora, Pedro foi o unico valente para avanzar a raina e do reino. Peter tina unha lanza dourada feita e tina un feitizo maxico poner na lanza que poderia matar a megera. A proxima ves que a bruxe veru a traves do ceo, Peter estaba esperando pore la. Peter tina todas as persoas e os seus animals esconderse nunha cova. Cando a bruxa do mai non ver calquera persoas ou animals, ela enfiou a cabeza a os ombros para for a de nube escura. Cando mirou arredor, Peter soubo vela e xogar sua lanza de ouro. Pedro feriu a bruxa e saiu correndo con medo, para nunca mais ser visto de novo. A fermosa raina e Peter viviu moi feliz para sempre. Como un recodatorio de ter sempre esperamos unha ponderosa fada fixo as nubes escuras nun viso dunha tempestade que se achega. A lanza de ouro converteuse en raios e os ruidos do coche a paso do Dragon tornouse o trono do tormenta. A fada dixo "Rember, tera felicidade tamen"…Durma agora o menu fillo.

There is a Scottish myth similar to this called "Conall and the Hag". It is of Celtic origin My Grandmother would tell me this story when I awoke through the night from horrible nightmares. She told it to me in Gaelic and the sound so soothing I was always able to go back to a peaceful sleep. I grew up in lots of abuse and my grandmother was my safe haven. I am not sure the translation is exact but it is the best I could do from her hand writing. Helen Dyck

Helen Dyck

MUSIC FROM THE GODS
IAN MANTLER

In a fit of boredom, Apollo left his place on Mount Olympus and took to wandering far afield in search of inspiration. When he arrived at the border of the lands of Asgard, Apollo continued onward out of curiosity. He had heard amongst the Romans that these lands contained gods like himself.

As he travelled into the strange land, he overheard of a place where the gods could be found called Valhalla. Eventually Apollo found a enormous golden hall that could only be Valhalla, with a beautiful golden tree in front of it, many huge doors, roof of thatched golden shields, rafters made of spears, and massive feasting rooms filled with warriors at leisure.

Apollo was considering whether to shoot the wolves and eagles that guarded the hall with his bow, when a messenger arrived and opened the ancient front gate for him. He was then ushered into the hall where the one named Odin presided.

The gods of Asgard seemed to snicker at their first glimpse of Apollo, finding his a strange sight. Apollo returned a look of distain at them in return. Odin, who kept one eye closed, called for silence and asked who he was.

Apollo declared his name and that he was the son of Zeus, before quickly adding that they would know of Zeus as Jupiter.

Odin distastefully agreed that they had heard of such gods

from the Roman invaders. With suspicion Odin then asked what the son of Jupiter wanted in this realm.

Apollo replied defensively that he was only looking for inspiration for his music and that it was Ares...who was Mars...who deal in war.

A god by the name of Thor then laughed, asking why one would seek inspiration within the heart of an enemy. Did Apollo value his music over his life?

Apollo retorted proudly that his music was the best in the world and that he had defeated all who would contest the title.

Thor laughed again and declared that he didn't need to play music. With his hammer, Mjolnir and its power over thunder and lightning, Thor could simply drown out whatever music Apollo would play. Apollo took out his lyre and argued that his music was greater than even the thunder. But Thor refused to back down from his declaration. Finally, Odin called for silence again and stated that a challenge had been declared. So Odin called for the best anvil be brought from the greatest forges of the dwarves so that Thor had a suitable place upon which to strike.

When an anvil was found and placed, Thor began constantly banging on it with Mjolnir. Apollo considered objecting that Thor had started too early. But then he realized that, deafening as Thor's strikes were, he might be able to work with the timing of the strikes to keep himself heard. So immediately after Thor's next strike, Apollo started playing his lyre. Still, even Apollo thought he might lose this challenge as he was forced to play louder and stronger just to be heard. He added his voice to his song, starting with a scream.

Thor quickly realized what Apollo was doing, so he changed the tempo of his strikes to try mess with Apollo's song. Apollo then changed the timing on his song to keep from being drowned out.

As the timing of the song was changed, the song itself changed. Then suddenly, Thor's strikes matched up to Apollo's song, adding to it in such a way that the song was not longer controlled by either Apollo or Thor any more. The song had become something else entirely. It was loud and hard, with a raw power that felt like it could shake the roots of the mountains themselves.

Even though no one in the hall could make themselves heard over the song and it felt uncontrolled and unrefined, they agreed that it was uniquely entertaining. So the gods of Valhalla let the song continue. Even Thor let the song continue, adding more strength and speed to his strikes to bring the song to a climax. Apollo followed suit, considering bringing back this new and impressive music to Mount Olympus. As such, he really pushed his limits to add more to the song.

But then the song became too powerful. It was then that it shook both Valhalla and the earth itself. Lava started to spray from cracks that appeared in the ground. The warriors in the feasting halls ran for their weapons, shouting about Ragnarok. It seemed as though the song was going to destroy Asgard. Even the gods started to panic and flee from the hall. Thor's hammering had too much momentum, he now struggled to stop his swings. Apollo realized that he would have to stop the song if he to keep it from destroying the world. So he did the only thing he could do. With the greatest regret he gave a final strum to his lyre, then threw it to the ground and broke it! At that same moment, Thor managed to bring his hammering to a halt with one final smash!

With that, the earthquake began to subside and the lava stopped flowing. Even the ears of the gods rang in the sudden relative silence. Apollo found that the he had become exhausted from his singing and playing. He gave out a last shout before passing out.

It had been many days when Apollo woke up again. It had been long enough that the gods of Asgard had managed to repair all the damage done to Valhalla. Somehow, one of them had even fixed Apollo's lyre to the point where even Apollo would swear that it had never been broken.

Recovering quickly, Apollo made a cautious study of the song and what had happened. He made a discussion of the matter in his final meeting with the gods of Asgard. Apollo concluded that he and Thor had competed and then played together so much and that the song had amplified their efforts to catastrophic proportions. Apollo believed that there was potential in this new form of music. However, the music was too uncontrollable, even for the lyre of Apollo. If there was a proper method to control the music, it would require a different, more refined set of instruments. With a hint of disappointment, Apollo summarized that using music would be too dangerous and should be left to maybe some other gods in some future time.

Although one or two shared Apollo's disappointment, all the gods of Asgard agreed that the music was too dangerous. Odin made a final judgement that it was impossible to judge a winner of the contest. Instead, they either swore or made one another swear to keep the song and the events surrounding it to be an absolute secret.

Apollo declared that he was returning home to Mount Olympus and that for the safety of the world, he would never set foot anywhere in the domain of Asgard ever again. To this news, the Odin bid him a grateful fair-well and Apollo left Valhalla. He returned to Mount Olympus with a reluctant to discuss his travels, but now inspired by the possibilities beyond.

ABOUT THE AUTHORS

Alexandra A. "Lexa" Cheshire lives in northern British Columbia, Canada. She is a wife and mother who enjoys to read and write fantasy and science fiction.

B. Heather Mantler is a lover of fairy tales and fables. Her home town is Prince George, British Columbia. Heather is always working on another story as she hopes to finish every story idea that she has written down.

Helen Dyck lives in Prince George, British Columbia.

Ian Mantler. He resides somewhere in Nanaimo. He says his contribution was inspired at the last minute.